The Napoleon House

The Napoleon House

Walter Schindler

Archon Books

First published 1989 as an Archon Book,
an imprint of The Shoe String Press, Inc.,
Hamden, Connecticut 06514

Printed in the United States of America

#1992/591

The paper used in this publication meets the minimum requirements
of American National Standard for Information Sciences—Permanence
of Paper for Printed Library Materials, ANSI Z39.48—1984.
∞

Schindler, Walter
The Napoleon House / Walter Schindler.
p.   cm.
ISBN 0–208–02251–1 (alk. paper).
ISBN 0–208–02268–6 (pbk. : alk. paper)
I. Title.
PS3569.C4965N37   1989
811'.54—dc20
89–34966
CIP

For Linda
Tes pas, enfants de mon silence

Contents

To the Possible Reader

If you are one
To sympathize
With what is here
Before your eyes,
And ask yourself
What you can do
To help the maker
Of a book that's new—
Then after you look,
Buy this, his book.
It has no purpose
But to please:
First, you, his reader
Who lend him time
To dream creating
Other rhyme;
And then his wife
Who is the Muse
That gives him life,
And misses sleep
When he wakes at night
To scribble until
He gets it right;

❋ ❋ ❋

She kept him in
His discipline
And out of law
Or medicine
(Until a second
Wind arose,
Promised new
Horizon glows,
And captain's orders
To his men,
He lifted anchor,
Sailed again)
And much he wrote
To please his friends,
For they can show
How Cicero
Should
Be understood,
And those great teachers
Who've taught more
Than he can ever
Thank them for,
And who allowed
His reckless mind
To grow more
And more refined.
But many a measure

❊ ❊ ❊

Only for pleasure
He wrote, and he wrote
But made erasure
For embarrassment.
His progress was slow
As a glacier
Over a continent.
Much he thought
He wrote for meaning
Didn't bear
A second screening.
So what is left,
Though not as old
As Horace wanted,
They're very cold
Ashes left
Of Shelley's ember,
The too familiar
Remnant of a mood
He can't remember.
But enough of all
This idle chatter—
It's just a good
Thing, the poetry
Does not matter.
It has no purpose
But to please:

❄ ❄ ❄

His father and mother,
Sister and brother,
Who guided trembling
Those first steps
On the green floor
Of memory.
And now, these
First steps
Of love and fear,
The marks of his
Necessity.

One

La dernière chose qu'on trouve
en faisant un ouvrage, est
de savoir celle qu'il faut
mettre la première.

The last thing we discover
in making a book
is the knowledge of what we
must put first.

—Pascal

The Invitation

The sun is rising: as the long, extended breeze
Breathes gently, slowly over vanquished limbs,
Limbs bathing in languor, weightless and still.
A smooth vibration or voluptuous tone
In and under the skin, in the cool flesh
Deep down, enchants and entrances the air. I am

Finding the way as I was found,
A newness ever flowing out of old,
Fresh and moving, as a new mountain stream
Guesses, by unknowing, where it's bound:

Take from me, as you would cup with both hands
A small pool of water from a limpid stream,
And drink, if you are thirsty. I am clear!
Look upon me, and through me to your own hands.

Mimesis

As a bird learns first on unknown wings to fly,
    So, trembling, heart—
    Outguess the art
To find your balance between love and fear.

But when the balance, wavering, leans to die,
    Then all will be death
    Until that breath
Comes on that no one feels, until it's near.

Aurora

(Torquato Tasso)

Here shiver waves,
There tremble leaves
To the morning breeze,
Birds desiring
In small young trees
Among green branches
Sing softest song—
Now smiles the dawn—
The sun appearing
In a sea of mirror
Is growing clearer,
The fields are fearing
Lost pearls of frost;
And the high mountains
In gold are drawn—
O graceful wanderer, Dawn—
Your news the wind is carrying
While you the wind's send
To parched hearts bringing
New life again.

The Rainbow

I

Like unexpected insight, thus
Bright mist you appear before us—
Rainbow—after so much rain,
Half-naked in the cloud, remain
The self-revealing accident
For those who fear their all is spent.

II

So, Noah, at the helm,
And all the happy animals below
Saw the disapproved world being bent
Under the flood.

Forty days and nights it rained,
The bobbing duck came not up again,
The earth was just a mass of mud
Buried in the ocean.

It took ten months to make it dry,
But since the ground was still quite wet
Noah made himself a bet
And took out of the ark an oar to try

❋ ❋ ❋

The ground: thus was Noah the first
To farm, he planted man's first vine.
How he lingered over the good taste of wine—
Something beyond water to sate his thirst!

Soon he felt a dizzy elation
And while his mind was turning in a reel
He grabbed something straight and made a wheel.
Wine and wheels! O civilization!

But that first drink went much too deep
And, off with his clothes, he wept himself to sleep.

There he opened his mind to a dream
In which God appeared and said: "Noah,
I have decided this flood is my last
Experiment; now we have only the past.

"Man is *it*—no more revision.
But I have set my bow in the cloud to give
Those who have a difficult decision
A sign about the life that they should live.

"My bow will appear to those who are set
On the right course; it will appear even

❊   ❊   ❊

When they are most confused, and most upset.
Pray, therefore, that they look to heaven."

III
"Is still your promise good?"
Asked Noah when he awoke.
For Noah had a notion
The world could only move
By God's emotion.
And again he spoke:
"Is still your promise good?"

IV
O Rainbow, you exist, and you exit
By perspective—
                    Seasoned survivor,
Elusive sight!
When your colorful rite
Appears semispherical,
How much meaning makes it
A miracle?

An Evening Song

As voices touch
By being still
When night is long
And time is slow,

And imperfection
Of the heart
Pervades the scene
And plays each part,

As minds reflect,
As paths begin,
A blessing comes
Of deep content,

The human touch
Upon an instrument.

Love's Dream Is Being Awake

Dreaming making love in the middle of the night,
Dream awakened lovers in a haze of light
Found dreaming making love fading into sight,
Waking, making love in the middle of the night.

Epithalamion

Happiness—and the Pacific Ocean—
Join in waves of joyous motion—
With pines in mist—
On shores just kissed—
The spray is the rainbow of emotion.

>   *Each can in the other see*
>   *His infant of identity.*

The sun shines ancient, happy world!
When gold horizons are unfurled,
Odysseus shall see
Penelope
In swimming eyes of happiness-wide-world.

>   *Each can in the other see*
>   *Her infant of identity.*

No single world can be profound
Until the leaves of love are bound
(As sight to sun)
All to one:
Searching man and woman now are found.

>   *Each can in the other see*
>   *One infant of identity.*

The Ark of Being

The being after which we inquire
is almost like nothing . . .
—Heidegger

Afloat upon the themeless sea
Without an image to be seen
He heard the music of again
Drift out upon the verge of be—

Then the sail that saves the wind
He lifted fast and prayed as fast—
Confusing music from all fears,
He lashed his heart to solid mast.

As if each moment of his life
Had been a tiger to be kept,
He saved it and what might have been—
Its silent mate that watched and wept.

Afloat upon the themeless sea
Without an image to be seen
Captain Silence waits upon
The storm of unbegun, unseen—

❅　❅　❅

The ark of being threads along
The high abyss, the flood of Now,
All past existence in its wake,
Becoming at the prow.

Vast created stars appear
To guide the sextant ship upon
The surface of the black blank flood
Into the illusion of the dawn.

Each failed world now is stored below
In corridors of the massive ark,
Empty cells await the ones
Found floating on the endless dark.

"Nothing left for God to be
But good, now that creation's blank"
So say the simple crew on watch
For rainbows, islands, cause to thank—

Now all is still upon the dark
As if the sky were Nothingness,
As if the flood below were all
The tears of God, forever less.

❋ ❋ ❋

The wind is down, the sky is dark,
The ocean calm and vastly wide,
No days or nights, no sun, no lights
Except the starlight on the tide.

"Where is the Captain?" ask the crew:
"Where's the Captain?" comes the cry
As if to ask the purpose now,
The rumor floods each mind with: "Why?"

Unknown to crew, the Captain's down
Below in cabin, taut in trance,
That All—All—has come to Nothing
And only Nothing has a chance.

"This is the end, the rumor's true—
No signal's come from God above.
We sailed the blackest deepest sea
Without the tinge of light of love."

Without the courage to begin
Without the sign, without the grace,
Captain Silence sat alone
A Blank upon his face.

Then into mind a voice returned
And in his heart a new sun burned:

✳ ✳ ✳

"Without the courage to begin
Without the sign, without the grace,
You can not drain the dead world out
Or let the New World in.

"The New World waits beyond the next
Dark Shadow of the Infinite—
Sail it by without a thought,
There's really Nothing in it.

"Beyond, I wait in New World time,
Watching, loving, knowing, seeing,
Only here as the Nothingness
That clouds, surrounds, and moves all Being."

The Captain rose and took the helm,
The Shadow of the Infinite
Flew by at instant of command!
(There really was Nothing in it!)

The vast horizon into view
Came reappearing red and blue,
And yellow, green, and all the colors
Of the ancient rainbow and the New.

Two

Animum debes mutare, non caelum.

—Seneca

Prayer at the Beginning of the Day

Great golden sun, arising in the sky,
Grant that I may look upon your day
Without regret and with a golden eye—
Grant that I will learn to love more deeply
The few among us that can be loved
Gracefully.

    Outside, the breaking haze
Suggests that it is possible
That this world is still possible—
May we who are its strangers and its guests
Learn to speak clearly in the stations
Of employment, where all are estranged—
You who are the Father of our times,
Firming up the phantasmagoria
Of the foggy world outside our window,
Lending the air of reality to the air we breathe,
You are the breaking distance of our secret longing
And the golden light of grand illusions.

The Train at Orbetello

We eat the pasta, drink the wine,
And sleep much in between;
The home we know's a symbol,
A rut of what we have not seen.

Thus some leave town for anywhere
Changing only place by name,
And some leave death for life and time
Feeling just the same.

For each will twist the possible
To change its name to true,
To catch a fallen visible
And pocket chance of blue.

Rounded skies enclose our worlds
In infinite regress;
A madman stops a stranger
With nothing to express.

Stand still at the station,
Watch the trains boom by,
Belting instant backward
To realized goodbye.

Les Pas

(Paul Valéry)

Your footsteps, the children of my silence,
Slowly, as if a saint's, appear.
Toward the bed where I am keeping vigil
They move, hushed and clear.

Pure being, shadow of divinity,
Your footsteps are made fresh, and with care!
O gods! . . . all the gifts I can imagine
Come and stand on those feet, so bare!

If, with those lips that I have sought,
You are preparing to appease
My one living thought
With the nourishment of a kiss,

Then do not hurry this gentle art,
Where the sweetness is in being, but not yet,
For my life has been only my waiting for you,
And your footsteps were the measure of my beating heart.

The Napoleon House

All that we have been,
All that we have seen,
Persuades us to begin
To drink contented and serene,

To drink and to remember
Our walk beneath night sky,
Forgetting the days dismembered
When meaning blanched the eye.

Though nothing stays the same
On these old city blocks,
The past's rekindled at the flame:
Wild Turkey on the rocks!

The past is good on Chartres Street
And good beneath the moon,
The future's only infinite
And always much too soon.

Let's keep the pain that's flowering
From fountains and from friends,
To teach the one live truth:
To love where meaning ends.

❋ ❋ ❋

For what could each have known
To boast how he stood at the brink—
When no one in this world
Has time enough to think?

Forgive us the arrogant pretense
Of youth gone mad with thought,
For the memory's proved more true
Than other fads we've bought,

And nothing we can say,
Nothing we can foresee,
Separates us from this place
Of lasting dignity.

New Orleans, 1975

To His Old Electric Fan

New Orleans

Old electric fan, my summer companion
In this hot room, while the day outside is burning—
Turn this humid air to a soft, cool breeze,
Spinning out just a visiting breath of wind,
Turning, spinning, just as before, returning—
Tell the winds to visit me, tell them I wait.
Though old, you have not broken yet
Or even stuttered, all these summers.
Smooth as silk you have cooled and calmed the wind.

Old eccentric fan, just as you are,
Help the winds to come to me, show them where I am.
Encourage them for my sake, for the sake
Of my face. Lure them if you can
With the curving of your changing hand,
Dizzy them if you must with promises—
But satisfy this burning, deepening within.
Help the winds to find me—gently guide them here—
I wait here watching the ease with which you spin.

❅ ❅ ❅

I am only now what I usually am,
Mumbling what I know, and nothing echoes.
I think I try to think
That these deserts of silence are deserved,
That I would not drink
The new water flowing like a calm wind.
I repeat over and over again:
If summer can turn day past day
Through the silence of the heaven,
Nothing of the world need be said today.

Interstate

Leaving now the floating silted city
Waiting in the swamplight for the sun,
Streaming down the dawnrose gray of miles,
The open road
Opens, like the old explorer's Nile,
Into the vast entanglement of nature,
Like a smooth curve into infinity
(Nothing in the endless landscape tells us
We are not in infinity,
The only travelers on this road,
Our truck the only visible trace of time)

In the golden light
The road slides like honey into the wilderness,
Bedding down the wild grass dream of trees,
From the hot crickets of Alabama
To the luminous owl-eyes of Maine,
Astonished at the vast unrelatedness
Chained by being—

Interstate—interpenetrate—
Much of the land still belongs
To wonder unconfused by a song,

❋ ❋ ❋

Or the human touch of right and wrong,
And to the wild, excited child,
Jumping up in high surprise,
        Wanting only the world
        To blossom in his eyes.

Cross Country

i

When first I came upon iambic dreams
The world was filled with adjectives and words
Were dreaming of their being here. Here

I fell out of the luxury of falling
Out of the dream of being
Within the realm of knowing—

Once more into the search,
Into the restless leaves of leaving late,
Wakened by the thought of travel interstate.

Intertwine the tangled roots of highway's land?
Daring the distance to revisit the dream,
California sunning time and waiting there

Like the last hope of a golden horizon,
A second chance, a second time, I begin
Not knowing the cost, at end, of fuel, horizon gazing.

ii

Leaving Boston, like the New World cracked open
The spirit rises moving ribbon-like

Westward, deserting the embattled Bostonian
To the tortured narrow tilted streets
Of jilted, pride-borne, generous Boston:
Rude roughhouse rednecks and flabby
Gabby women, buttressing distressed Irishmen,
Insolvent taxis and pot-hole shot-through streets
Of disappearing true-descendant trusted Boston:

Penniless in sunset, I go, with a pod of never-
Planted, Plymouth's urgent seed.

Muses—inspire, where educators train,
Strain to prop the ivy-strangled mind
In the language-tangled hothouse
Of civilization. The dull road stains the eye
With gray, the sun road flares
The detail-scorched memory.
But when I left, soft-glowing red drizzle-
Glazed brick seemed to forgive all the changes
And the halting steps and faltering beginning.
All at once the air seemed fresh again,
The new rain fell over and over—
So when Mohawk Valley like a primitive god
Flashed lightning, out of dark May clouds
Hurled mountainous rain, and hail thick
With crushed ice dropped like mud, draping windshields
And halting cars and trucks

* * *

33

Like nineteenth-century horses
Stalled in the delirium of the future,
The peace that everyone thinks wisdom brings
Descended on me, but it was not wisdom—
It was nearness to death and to you.

iii

Driving toward Niagara from the back of the Falls,
The anxious eye sees nothing but a calm
Sheeted river drowsing, a calm-crazed crawl.

When water's white breath quickens, the portent comes too late:
At the end of the downwinding river's roll,
Like the dying vortex in the shaman's cry,

Earthquake-struck the heart's high waters breaking unbounded let
Fall all halting walls against the waters, altars heaving
Broken heaven upon heaven,

The Thunder of Waters arching the aura of stone,
Spanning across the congressed layers of history,
Pouring rushing reaching failing forging forgotten words—

But on the weather-breaking beaten back of time,
Like steam from summer rain, or bow from fall of rain,
The cloud out of Niagara ascends a cloud of sky.

❋ ❋ ❋

iv

In the blue mist of morning, still before daybreak,
The serenity of long Canadian farms
Rendered the ambition-haunted frustration-gaunt
Encircled lost tribes
Moments in the waterfall—

In the peace of Ontario countryside,
The uncertainty of America came close—
Its faltering confidence came buzzing about my ear.

Back in Michigan, the road running south
Abandoned farms and de-flagged mail-boxes,
The beet-red barns demystified by rain and sun,
A wind stained wood framed
Windows of regret.

v

    Crossing Lake Michigan
To Manitowoc, the clouds broke and the gray cried
And language fell like rain. When the sky
Cleared and the sun returned, word-beaten
Language languished in the circular sea.
Now waves wash behind us
Meaningless metaphors: the world is crazed and still.

❄   ❄   ❄

But silent into fog-drift without warning
Sudden glare strains all directions blank—
No sky, no lake, no shore, but a blur all blinding
The bound eye searchless, stunned behind its lid
Of stark white haze like darkness, but light.
At last the ferry warning ferrets out
A sound within the fog, another lost,
That long low vowel lingering out its animal reply,
A language borne in a single note upon a single sea
Holding and holding over its distant breath:

 Here—
 To be
 Here—
 In the wake of now—
 Blind
 Being—
 And here—
 To be present,
 To be living and breathing,
 To be in and above and out and back
 Floating like a fire in a pyromaniac world,
 But swimming now without a sight of shore—
 Wandering from there to here, and waiting,
 Waiting from then to now, and learning
 Alone, in the stillness of the fog,
 Almost how to see, to see through hearing,

❋ ❋ ❋

Almost almost knowing
Deeper and deeper how to know,
Seeing time in the drift of dream of drift,
Hearing space in the hallowed fog of mind,
No longer being here, but becoming,
Moving as if in the one direction known—
Almost as if living in the thought of God—
Almost as if living near God—

Even if forever foreclosed—
If almost forgotten—
But interwoven—
Like the pen waiting and watching the words it writes
And the man writing and thinking the words he now watches.

vi

Sleeping near the bridge-pass at La Crosse,
All night long I dream
Of this continent-dividing river,
And of children finding a way across upstream.

And questions traversing the Mississippi River
Come and go, slow-dancing until dawn,
Or playing just a made-up children's game
Which does not start, until I am gone:

❇ ❇ ❇

Why do we read?
Why do we write?
Why do we read what we write?
A second time?

We're going West where no one knows
A scholar in the wintertime,
A mind chilled to a point of ice
New England pure and still.

Though no one knows what rivers think at sunrise,
The rules have told us boldly not to care,
To bathe quietly like an invalid in the wells of being,
Noting not the voice that's never there.

Dangling by a handgrip off a ledge
Of paper, the mysterious climber, the daresman
Now a parody? Out of urban thought and paradox
A cleaner sun reclaims this sifted land

And the invisible current of the river flowing
Onward and forward and moving forever back
To the place where, leaving once, I was born.
Why do we keep reading when we know we're going blind?

❉ ❉ ❉

vii

As straight and flat as the flattest tile of flatland,
The South Dakota hog-heaven of corn-heaving earth
Stretched out of sight.
                        Fighting high winds, an eagle
Whose sight without warning swept secondless
Disdained the monotonous road, the strong wings
Held out displayed a photographic moment.

Nothing happened for an hour after that.

A hastily constructed sign read at the border:
    Nothing comes out of South Dakota
    That doesn't go in, first.

viii

Over another barren hilltop of Wyoming,
Without a desert flower for the eye,
A sandy blank of nowhere spotted with sagebrush,
Like a mind purged of everything but dredge,
And then another dirt Wyoming pile, a hillside
Hiding another bare brown hill,
And then, over the last perhaps—

❋ ❋ ❋

On the distant horizon, at second glance, not clouds
But spectral snow of mountains disbelieved at first,
The far-off peaks of orange-tint horizon's vast
Refractions of an infinite cut in bronze—

Thus driving toward the last dream of Olympus,
Climbing clanking godward on a myth of gasoline,
The slow sloping at the base turned and circled
Learning curving holding slanting roads—
Declining only to surge
Meandering again—
But in the end and without loss of longing
At the top of the last loop
Across the highest arch,
Powder River Pass six feet deep in snow,
With no one in the world but a desperate dream of me,
I walked breathing slow first steps, then ran and ran—
Wild as Wordsworth in Switzerland,
As if nothing depended on poetry:

> *To forget the life and to forget the text,*
> *Like traveling without a book*
> *And hearing the words before remembering them,*

❀   ❀   ❀

To become lost in those words, as in the aura
Of standing on this mountain pass at sunset,
And to see, from the center, the complete horizon

Around us—a ring with a burning stone.

ix

High in wooded mountains
Yet near the magma's heat
Amid impulsive steams
And streams,
Encircled glory comes
To the morning glory pool,
Fed from water's heated dreams
Flowing underground:
Where no man knows the sound
Of his own voice, awakening
The rhythm of his breath,
Cadencing the hour
Of freedom and power,
Or sees his name drop silent in the pool—

Entering the cavern of the language
Sunlight fractions water blue and green,
Green for earth and blue for sky,
Green for hearing, and blue for sight,
Flooding all the spectrum in between—

❊   ❊   ❊

Here, the voice of being
Comes to be heard, thus
No one knows the wisdom
This voice brings—

Because sheltered in hurt or happiness,
Sheltered in the calm of a listless eye,
None will range to break the distance
Difficulty brings—

Like poise on the brink of failure,
Sunset under prism of the storm,

Truth breaks horizons manifold and plenty,
Truth pools the morning being brings.

x

Walking red roads as almost mist the light rain winnowed down,
Watching it muddle meanings in the mud, meandering,
I took the trail that broke from sight road-weary drivers take
Who rather would go walking in the showers of slow rain
Than hide in highway taverns, in civilized refrain.
Then, on one pond, the drop-by-drop that thistled down
The leaf, stirred the sheen that only pools of myth can make.
Glancing down, I see the face that I forget by wandering:

❉   ❉   ❉

Why do you always need
A walk in sad weather
To know the clay
Inside you must remain,
That the reddest must
Be kneaded most
To ever much
Refabricate that brain?
So strike a pose
You want preserved,
Even in this weather,
And those who do not see
Shall witness blind
What clumsy hands can strain to be,
Though showers fall again,
As long as hands of clay
Shall long to mold
The sculpture of a man
Standing in the rain.

xi

Rock once stood a symbol of eternity,
But knowledge of the rising-falling earth
Rendered even rock
And ancient sunlit shapes of stone
An obsolescent brown adobe dream.
Now all who come the burning road for visionary chance

❋   ❋   ❋

Stand frozen at the sight of change
That turns the dream of gods
To images of dream.

For thus, in the desert,
In the mountains,
Where once a stream divided, running west, running south,
Red Rocks Standing Like Men
Borrow the glance of an unknown metaphor
From the prism of similitude: the waking trance
Of human faces seen with human eyes—
A grand Rodin sculpture of a movement
Of history, the forces and the furies
Frozen like dusted ice inchoate melting
Halted between rude time and a red rhymeless sunset.

xii

A desert, an ocean, a few worn words remain:
Extant words, incessant care,
Survivors on the thoroughfare
Of tradition's dream, dream's child, child's fantasy:

Steering through Mojave, towels held to the wheel
Too hot to hold, hands too fast bead sweat
To grip the slippery wheel without those towels (dripping wet):

❋ ❋ ❋

In the desert it is possible
To watch yourself thinking
In the distance: look
At the landscape beat
Like a giant crusted heart,
The air turning swirling
Twisted shapes, the muted
Tree brush standing
Like silent scattered stone.
In the desert we are almost
Nonexisting, hugging close
The heart-pulse of uncertain
Seeing there, gasping for
The wet-edged line of being,
Our choking voices,
Our dazed out sight beyond,
Gagged and blind.
Now imagine the heart stop, and time
Burn all being out of mind—

In reverie my household gods, clutched and carried Westward
In the pocket of my travel bag, mock me steaming:
"In time your burdened words may learn to stand,
But not now, not now: you come too early, yet came too late;
In time, yet without time, you strain your hand,
Just as American imagination
So quick to cross the continent, slowly finds the land."

❊ ❊ ❊

At last, as the sunset softening
Of the glare-strained day began,
I reached the end at the floating edge of ocean
And a City on the desert by the water—
Mirage of freeways, buildings, deathless palms,
Bending for air as a sea breeze withers inland
Into heat—

> *The spirit labors near the sea*
> *To make a garden wilderness*
> *Within adobe cloisters rise,*
> *Like half-built Spanish missions*
> *Planting the dream of Paradise.*

> *At last, those flowers will grow,*
> *And the green will be flourishing,*
> *Within the limits of the sun,*
> *As if nothing had been labor*
> *When all the work is done.*

So much a song for the angels ground
Is ground into dust,
Unless the deep horizon red at the smog-smeared edge of sky
Inspires the hope of a marriage hymn
Uniting earth and paradise.

❋　❋　❋

As if on this beach a man without a century
Held his arms stretched out like a cross,
Accepting nothing but the thought
Of what is possible,
And giving all he has for nothing less—

Who knows when
Whether part of us
Will ever reach a shore of content,
Or a strain
Of longed-for mastered music
Will leave us at rest or rent?

Who knows when
What the meaning is
Shall break from the potter's hand,
And the work
Of the earth-molding laborer
In the image of dying shall stand?

Interlude

John Milton
Never stayed in a Hilton
Hotel:
It was just as well.

—W. H. Auden

Interlude

Come, reader, let's take a rest.
Serious efforts are seldom best.
Blindness comes from too much reading,
As accidents from reckless speeding.
Nothing more profound's been said
Than: "Let's spend this day in bed."

In bed are man
And woman brought
Together to
The joy they sought.

In bed is wisdom
Made divine
As he knows best
Who drinks her wine.

In bed is seen
That all man's search
Which brought him
to
His present perch

❋ ❋ ❋

Has nothing but
Delusion been,
And idleness
Without the sin.

To bed, therefore,
Go right away
And leave this book
For another day.

Three

Noi eravam lunghesso mare ancora,
come gente che pensa a suo cammino,
che va col cuore e col corpo dimora.

We were alongside the ocean, still,
Like people who ponder on their way,
Who go in their hearts, but in their legs delay.

—Dante

On Teaching a Child to Read

I hesitate to teach you, happy child,
To read the words your eyes are fabled with,
To open the doors to neverending meaning
That never quite all interconnects so well
The problem of pain and the dream of happiness
That never seems enough, except in dreams.
What the words will mean, I think I know
But can not tell how words can mean, or why,
Or help you know who gave this perilous gift
Of breaking into sound and sense alone.

Not Reading in the Garden

Open the book
And look:
You can not read
Your work has so exhausted you

The camellia leaves are rich and dark
The sun is quiet, clear and bright

At the center of the world
Is a book that is not being read
With leaves that are always open

Turn the pages
Of the sages:
The print is black and quiet,
You can see letters,
Word-seeming arrangements, lines
That might have a meaning if read

In this centrifugal unguided century
We are working in the stasis of a dream
For the books we can remember
To have been ourselves, and are ourselves
On the day when once again
We lift the book, open the leaves,
See word-seeming words, and read.

At the Hotel La Valencia

From all the places, all the dreams
I have fled from you—Muse—
From the mountains and streams
To where all landscapes fuse—

In the bluest waters of the deepest sea
From out the window of this pink hotel—
I came to find lost poetry
Without a story or a truth to tell—

Alone in a room with a view—
With little of me and none of you—
I did not have to die to live,
You did not have to love to give—

All we needed was to bet our soul
On a throw of dice, the one-time roll,
And pray them seven as we spellbound see:
Now—it is now—it is you—it is me

Waterfall Vision at Villa d'Este

To see the world through a veil of water
Under a falling hope of sight,
Behind the wall and still within the dream—

Through patch of cloud and passing leaves in flight
Sunburst rivets every drop of stream
And all those faces faceless next to one—

To see her, then to know how here, alone,
We watch for all we love through water,
Calling this the world, and all the world of light.

The Commute

Then each day was new,
Now the dawn is old,
Riding a bus two hours a day,
Knowing the road is cold.

I can not think,
I am not free,
But the bus runs humming
And I can see:

The buildings' horizon,
Miraculous bay,
And in and out of the fog,
A hidden way.

So keep me lost in tradition,
Keep my eyes lost on the sea,
Take away wandering ambition,
I am bound by the threshold to be.

❋ ❋ ❋

Keep me lost in the ordinary everlasting,
In the kindness of all this unknown.
I've surprised myself: I am happy
When this is all I own.

Berkeley–San Francisco,
1974

Sunset and Evening
at the Berkeley Rose Garden

I

Bright rose of sun,
The day's work is done,
And here, a stream
Out of its dream
From under the ground
Opens in air
Without a sound,
Without a care.
It is going
Under this bridge
Toward sunset flowing
Toward Golden Gate Bridge,
And two of us are talking
As if a dream has just created us,
As if words had not existed until then.

II
A wind is rising from the distant fires,
There is silence in the garden of the stars,
And young ambition talks
Against the wind and this cold night of stars—

❋ ❋ ❋

All things must change—
Say the stars darkening—
Before you may experience
Even once this joy again.

Visions of Van Gogh

I

> *. . . suppose that his dreams and the*
> *visions of his imagination spoke*
> *no more and that every tongue*
> *and every sign and all that is*
> *transient grew silent . . .*
>   St. Augustine

Death of father, father of death
Dark glow dark green dark faces of
Potatoes, a lost supper—

Tobacco spins away this night of rest,
And I do not complain.
I will write Theo
Who has understood my silence.

When stillness of the soul concedes
Satisfaction with images,
When the paint is dry and I am dead,
I breathe and as I breathe the wonder is
I do not disappear

❊   ❊   ❊

But because life has endowed
These sullen ashes, my eyes,
In the rising sun of every day
I am born—

Star, who doubted your burning
Because of the infinite dark?

In the deep cold heart of winter coal,
A preacher among miners in the Borinage—
I rose with the cloud-locked sun from distant night,
And a voice broke out from the dim morning:

Go beyond the conversion of mankind,
Leave the hopeless task of the hopeless
To the weary and the kindest hearts
Of every generation that blossom in the winter chill
To find a cause to die in and long to make
A world to believe—

You are an improbable artist, Vincent; yet
You must paint for those who have fainted and fallen,
The petals of flowers unseen,
The leaves of trees in another world's autumn,
The eyes of another man's dream.

※　※　※

Dark glow dark green
Circle of homage and the dust of shoes—
Out of the ashes and the images, there remain
Faces of courtesy in the lamplight of dream—

The time to work does not return.

No food for two days—but coffee and sweat—
All reverie in hunger and dream of sleep—
It's the world that strains us outside hope
But the straining of all our desire
Can not redeem the world as it is—
Love too often exceeds our nerves—
Father—teach us how a man becomes beautiful
By suffering, and the world itself satisfied by the pain.

The nights when I have not the strength to remember
What strength I have, I walk in the wind down
The streets of Arles and if the air is sewn
With secrets, I listen, quietly, as a length
Of wind lengthens and soothes my skin; I can
Imagine in the Alyscamps a man
No one knows, soiled like an old potato, hidden
In the riot of Provençal red roses, thinking
As the wind crowds leaves like the ghosts of Charon,
Of someone he has seen on the street only once:

❊　❊　❊

A face. And if it is mine, what can I say?
For when night comes, for both of us, the day
Is dream. Now I am alone with his presence
In a dream where he sleeps: imperfect and unknown,
Brother to the earth and the son of silence.

Tobacco spins away this night of rest,
And I do not complain.
I will write Theo
Who has understood my silence.

II

And his face is withheld from the knowing
And covers the winds with art
Hölderlin

A wind is on the graves, lost with the day
In the ground or the stone: Nothing awaits them.
The leaves at fall, parchment papers, curled,
Dispersed, like memories, into desperation.
As the long breeze lengthens, the sense of air stirs
Beneath the skin and
Over the fatal tablets of their final aspiration.
Wind
Over the graves, as the leaves scatter
Scattered leaves,
A promise follows the air whirling nowhere

❋ ❋ ❋

The things of the world tremble
On the edge of revelation, vibrate
In a fragile light, yet seem
In the end not to move at all
From their transparent prisons—
A teasing glowfly
    in a dark garden,
A limpid ray of light
    from a lingering sun,
A gasp of air
    from a drowning star.

Being itself is clear
In the clarity of the air;
Warm, in the warmth of the blood
(It is there)
In time it wells up within
And out to the point of a tear

    under the sun.

    Under the sun

Mere being may amaze me, whirling
In the fall of time, passing
To a new, quiet man—
Who will wait to recover
To dare to be dazed again.

✳ ✳ ✳

And even our dreams

Are dreams,
I leaned above the water, staring in the water
Clean as my face was not and not as my eyes were—
What is cleanness when a face can feel no rain?
Is the wind enough to brush the dust away?

Wind

Over the graves, as the leaves scatter
Scattered leaves,
A promise follows the air
Whirling nowhere

III

Commune with your own heart upon your bed, and
be still
Psalm 4

This is the night of the world,
Where the stars are like cities in a foggy sky,
Or boating lights seen from a bridge.

Waiting here in the night watch—
In the blindness of starlight—
Close—my eyes—

❄ ❄ ❄

Let light in—
Let sprinkled light between your lids
See and see not light dark light—
In time the tenuous lids can filter
Figures blue in patterns dancing
You see them as you make them as you almost dream
You think this as you watch your ballerinas masterful
Yet you can not move as these dolls do—
They would dance forever were your lids not tired already—
There are partners among them and they are polite
They are oblivious to themselves as you can not be
Because they do not lie still: See
And see not

I have walked this earth for thirty years—
But returning from Saintes-Maries-de-la-Mer
Where color bleeds from the heart of things
And the sun is the fountain of the sea
I have come to see
That what I most want to paint
Has not yet been seen—
The green, red and blue boats
Are fields of flowers,
A little town is surrounded by hills
Covered with yellow and purple flowers
Like a Japanese dream.

❋ ❋ ❋

And the cathedral stands at Chartres,
While far off in a rosegray twilight
The white stones on the shore lie still.

I would write Theo. Theo,

Ideas of an unknown land
Are like the shadings of your mother's eyes,
If you had not been born.

What is there to express
But what we are not?
How can you forgive
These abstract ecstasies
When I am unkind to you?
How can I express to you
The love that overwhelms me?

I could not believe it, I thought,
I could not think it, I believed,
But the vision of the torture of the innocent—
The vision of the riders in their merciless arc—
The vision of the muted alone in the shafts—

Love is everywhere powerless,
Love and power, interlocked and opposed—
All things are falling from us

✸ ✸ ✸

And nowhere is the circle closed—
When the clouds come,
    each man is heavenward,
      yet the clouds
Depart; and resolve is broken; and again
The fog suffers, the winds are chained
There is nothing yet
There is nothing, yet
There is—

After the mines and the pilgrims there,
And a broken vocation—
A prayer stopped dead at the middle of a word—
None can aspire without the context of heaven,
None can aspire, none can know
The young man in the coal mine, his soot-cough breathing
At the bottom of the world
His ears hear the silence at the end of words,
The breaking of rock, the dust fall, the quiet—
No, none could forgive, there, none could know,
Without the context no one could think
The air must be there if only to frustrate
The clarity possible because we can not see—

Cover calm down slow where under sleep
Out of window try I wander day-old eyes
And wonder is the world if painted on the pane

❄ ❄ ❄

Or dream is night if black holes at the back
Of night where what if whirled of darkness what
Rivers terror prevent all going there where
Have I come what from what done if only time is won—
Remember there—travel then—only dream

IV

O my soul, it is just your
unknowingness that I need
Tertullian

At the least bend of light, shall I end my darkness?
I am the last of it, and lie here dreaming
The colors of a morning to dare the day's call.
The lost, toss off; hold off the bleak walls,
The last are leaving; breathe now; begin—

Come, Vincent, and declare
The beauty of this day,
Which insists the glory
Of a simpler kingdom.

Here, the fragile things
The violent sun has spared
And patience has delivered,
Give thanks to silent air,
And homage to the calming wind,

❆ ❆ ❆

Thanking soft earth, the slow river
And the quiet streams.
Accept, accept all this.
The day has opened:

> *I have walked with the father of my being*
> *I have slept in the being of my love*

Theo, if I write to you,
Do I speak to myself, or to no one, or to God?

Why is it when I am alone in my mind
And hear God listening behind the emptiness
Like the neverending surface of a wall,
Why is it that I fear Him, forgetting Love?
Why in the dark unknown do we run in fear, not joy?
I paint the dreams of happiness and love
But when my ear is to the wall
All my hope is all to hold the fibre of my being one
And keep the calm from rending me apart.

Standing on the verge of standing still,
The wonder breathes, freezes breath and chill—

I cast out of my mind into the painting itself:

✳ ✳ ✳

The tortured shapes of the olive tree
In winter, grey in meaning,
Wait above in the raw verdure,

And just before spring, when the air is clear
After long rain, still, those chill shapes
Are waiting alone in the new found sun—

I wake from sleep as if outside of life—
Circling the edges of the stars
With trembling hands—
And yet each night I last until the morning

V

Day unto day uttereth speech,
and night unto night sheweth knowledge.
There is no speech nor language
where their voice is not heard.
Psalm 19

No voice opposes mine. I am alone.
The ear draws closer to itself, and hears:
The one low hum of a single being.

To have made many things that are unknown—

❄ ❄ ❄

Light is invisible
Where it has no object.
The eye is sighed with seeing.

The clarity of darkness between the stars—
    A motion without measure—
    World by world—
Moving in the mind of God
    Universe by universe—
    Star by star—
Darkness all knowing
Distant and near—
Father, forgive us our perspectives—

I want to give personality to olive trees
And give to them their suffering arms,
And, at the end of cypress swirls, exploding stars—
To give light back to the sun
And eternity to the sunflower
And of me to give to all all I have done—
Dabs of color on the rags of time—

Today whined the ghost of mistral:
Energy to canvas shaking—
Painting canvas bending in the shrieking blast—

❊ ❊ ❊

In day the wind, at night the peace
    of painting the stars,
Where there are no borders,
And unreal distances call us,
The timeless calm, the invisible dark,
A heaven of desolate suns.

As each day's torpor shades me
I am disowned by daylight,
But at night my blood's admiration burns
For the star, in the whirl of its silent spinning—

Is the way
Lost to love
The world?

As more battered and bold, as weaker and poorer I get,
The more I want to break all light
To brilliant color, in harmony, resplendent.

                    To reveal what is comforting
                    As music is comforting

My house I want to be the house of light for everyone—
In love's collage, all breaking true—

                    ❋ ❋ ❋

Deaf now in one ear
By my hand, but not my heart—
The intention of love
Is suffering punishment—
And my will in living
Is a blind man's art—

I walk, faceless, through a crowd
And see my face everywhere.
Am I no one, or everyone?
When we who are living
Can not speak of joy,
Why should the dead whisper?
We are as silent to them as they are to us.

You who survive
Are breathing the unutterable air,
Responsible for my life,
Mirrors of my breath,
My possibility. How can you forget this?

Where, where shall we find
And when, under what winter of snow,
A leaf of the sun?

❋ ❋ ❋

The gnarled trees wait,
     speechless grandfathers.
On their withered arms, the birds
Are unable to die.
An opening blossom, a tangle of hawthorn,
Moss, the hanging of time, frozen voices—

We become
All night and day
The bridges and the ships
Pass waves in eyeless water
We pass
Through streets
Alive with flowers, hidden in fears
Through boulevards and avenues
We live and move and have our being
On paths without a forest
Over hills no one can see behind
Aspiring in houses of lust
To trust of dreams
And all of this our sleep
Ascends to the calm of moon,
And now and then
To the dream of the sower in the sun—
Is this one—
Where beyond all guess—
Is the world—
Whirled wordless—
Wordless

Four

Als strömte von den alten, stillen Mauern
  Mein Leben flutend und verklärt herein.

. . . As if from these ancient, silent walls
My life, transformed, were flowing back to me.

—Hugo von Hofmannsthal
(translated by
Michael Hamburger)

Invocation

Words, I need you—
Come and rest
Upon my voice—
Words, mean something
As if meaning
All came true.

Words, be a part
Of the voice that humbly
Speaks for you
And asks the question
Only you can answer.

Guido Cavalcanti in Exile
(Translated from his Italian)

Because I do not hope ever to return,
O little song, to Tuscany,
You go there, instead of me,
Light and soft go, and find my lady,
Who in heart-deep courtesy
Will greet you as a longed-for guest.

You will bring her the news of my sighs,
Full of steep pain and deep fear;
But make sure no one sees you
Who's suspicious of our gentleness,
For then you will be harassed,
And she, so displeased,
It will mean my torment
Lasts until my death,
And even then—
Tears and grief again.

You can feel, O little song, that death
Has me gripped so tight that life is leaving;
You can sense how my heart shakes

❊ ❊ ❊

Because of what my every instinct fears.
So much of me is already destroyed
That I can't suffer more, and still be.
If you would help me,
I beg you this favor:
Take my soul with you
When it has left my heart.

O little song, into your confidence
I entrust this soul that trembles.
Take it with you
(It was thus devoted)
To that lovely lady
To whom I send you.
O little song, tell her with sighs
When you kneel before her:
"This, your servant, comes here to stay with you,
Departed from him who was the servant of love."

You—my own voice—bewildered and weak,
That come weeping from this heart that grieves,
Go with my soul and with this little song
And speak of how my mind is destroyed.
There, you will find a woman so pleasing
And of so sweet a mind
That it will be your whole delight
To stay with her always.
O my soul, adore her
In all her worth forever.

The Snow Fall

White and delicate and delicately falling,
White and small and lightly in the wind
They sift innumerable spaces of the light and dark
As they fall in the way that they learn to fall,
Bowing with a soft distress,
   And almost lifting their way down;
Fragments like the dust beside the Parthenon
Or broken museal columns
Of deadened Dresden: there is nothing that stays.
In a dead fall, there are words that spell, like leaves,
Their sacrifice; there are worlds that freeze
In a thought, in a wish, in a lost emotion,
Worlds that speak in one word spoken.

   Again the memory of the crude passage,
And the sudden knowledge, like a voice unknown:
The world is not dead, it has been forgotten.
   But where *ver perpetuum est*
But where the spring is perpetual,
A frantic mother looks and calls
For her lost daughter; and pausing
To rest on a desolate stone,
Whispers her disbelief and awe:
   She was of intricate things, the remnant;
   Of many tortured graces, the delicate fall.

The Warsaw Ghetto Uprising

I now no longer know, if God
Is growing in us, as Rilke said,
Or if God is so distant and unmoved
The universe is a fading and a cry

But nothing, out of all that is, can be
If no one can hear the never ending
In the darkness of all silent death
Dischordant cries of the crumbled Ashkenazim

Quivering like candles in the windows
Of the ghetto of our memories—
We who wish we could exist and know it
And crawl out of our disastrous skins

To find a flame to die in
And rise to find a world to believe.

The Dark Ages

Not until this stillness,
Not until standing in this cloister did I know

All those centuries of silence
And courtyards of flowers, fountains, and trees,
Meditative tombstones set in damp cloister walls,
Death surrounding life, waiting in harmony,
Like the isle of paradise under total eclipse
Waiting for the image of the sun.

No wonder then that time seemed timeless,
No wonder eternity gleamed in bright mosaic gold;
Little did they dream beyond their aspiration
And error, their rank and mystified humanity,
That ages hence would doubt the one meaning they knew—

The bell tolled out of the high campanile
And the air lengthened out each longing, dying sound,
But Anselm thought only about Being
Alive.

The Stone-All-Wall

Within the stony silent place
Between the fern rows God let be
I came upon the STONE-ALL-WALL
That squared my vision three by three

Two eyes upon the strongest reach
Three reasons bracing up the wall
Four limbs so coldest Life had gone
And then I heard the call

All without the rings of freedom
All within the stars of grace
Yet panic all the stony prison
Granite clutch of His embrace

Two eyes for freedom then I prayed
Three prayers for reasons waved like sea
Four minds upon the battlement
And motion moved so noiselessly

✳ ✳ ✳

As if the God who sat within
Had locked Himself within the stone
To dream away the universe
Into the infinite at last alone

As if beyond the silent place
Beyond the fern rows He let be
God found Himself a limit
Where all He meant was ALL-TO-BE

VI Centenario della Morte
di Giovanni Boccaccio

for John Freccero

Eternity, aeternitatis,
This day in Italy,
Once again without wanting to,
I've discovered what I want
(While the sun goes burning down the sky)
And seen Boccaccio's tower, where
Without our doubt of mystery
The aging scholar thought through the evening air.

The serene heaven's blessing now
Our profane world and his:
The green hills are waning into blue,
And this serene disappearing afternoon,
The people here are idle
Because there is nothing to do,
But wait for the changing of the sky.

✻ ✻ ✻

Certaldo is the kind
Of perfected disorderliness
You can find where the world has not changed,
Much like the Bay, Bay St. Louis,
The one I knew as a child—
Where the piers going into the hurricane
Grow silent in the late afternoon.

And this sun that sets afire
The whole horizon red,
This sun is the silence
That is changing the world,
Like the calm in the eye of the hurricane,
And the sun, is it falling
Behind that distant hill
Because our perspective has changed?

Certaldo, 1975

Hotel Dieu:
A Birthday Elegy for T. S. Eliot

I

Passing the glass-walled nursery in the corridor, I pause.

Still is the child
Behind the glass
That questions me with a stare.

Intoxicated veins flow
With the dark wine of the mother
To the heart,
like irresistible rivers to the sea.

The room is a garden
Grown with the gowns
Which cover us all.
Who will wake them now?

If I do not stand too close, I can see
My reflection in that glass.
Shall I preach to this ghost

❀ ❀ ❀

Or to those bald heads?
The indifferent, hopeful eyes in a hundred pews.
   Tremens factus sum ego et timeo
On the fresh skin, from the severing there,
The perpetual scar.
Lux perpetua luceat eis. After birth the bird
Falls from the nest, in the air attempts a cry to his world
And fails: beside the rotten pulp of fallen fruit.
In the dark hair of distant hills,
Branches are blasted in night's white lightning
Where death hides beneath the visionary flash.
At the beach, a wave rolls toward the castle-children,
Is defeated; but then reach forward
The long fingers of foam.

II

Why should I wipe my glasses clear
To see a blurred world?
        The path a man has come
Becomes only dust for sparrows
And the shadows
Lost in recurring dreams.
The path forward does not appear
Until it is taken
And the hollow foot presses the earth.

❀ ❀ ❀

The moment, alone, on the pier:
There is the flash, a fish
On lambent pinions, fluttering fins.
My reflection is disturbed . . .

   Is this the face, this face
So numbed by the insurgent terror
Of all that is possible?
This face of the speechless patient
Strapped to the moving table in the long corridor
As the ceiling changes above him from gray
To gray, and disinfectants flood the air,
The nurse smiles, distantly, to him locked
In the silence of his broken prayers. Endlessly rolling
On small grinding wheels of steel. Toward
The unparted waters . . .

   The analogies I want to construct
Will only constrict me. And all the naked words
In a nervous limbo,
When they see themselves in a mirror,
Become self-conscious and are afraid to speak.
Silent, they return to an older chaos; the duration
Of an awareness of no duration,
Has endured,
And ends.

❇ ❇ ❇

I remember the place, and the time
When eyes, locked in fright, foretold the world
Would divide our worlds.
But we stood in the garden
And would not move, like children.
And all around us rose the gloom
Of silence.

The desolate cry in the winter forest,
The bird's light song of the spring,
The hum and clatter, confusion of summer,
The dry rustle of autumn lament
Are the convoluted music of the seasons,
Of twirling tops and shifting faces,
Of disconsolate lands risen and sunk.
Dust and wind. Cloud and sun.
The river winds down to the sea.

III

The divinity of sorrows
Hovers in the air
The echo or idea of a passing chord,
Or the idea of the organ itself.
Tremens factus sum ego et timeo
Waiting for the new eyes
To cry from these cradles
(Amid the cries of sailors in a senseless storm)

❈　❈　❈

Is someone there?
I turn my gaze
Down the corridor. Empty. As the air.
Once, last night, I turned around from my desk: only
The ghostly dance of curtains in a drafty hall.
Further into the night, I heard in half-dream
   Two voices ascend from a land of dust:

"Does the wheat still stand in the field?"

"The stalks yet stand, barely.
They are rotting away, soon to fall,
Like old men who can no longer hear or feel.
And even if they could hear,
They would hear only the wind.
And if they could feel,
They would feel only the dryness of the air."

"No sign of spring?"

"Only the death of the old.
Not even the illusion of new things.
The days lengthen,
Darkly.
The nights shorten,
Bitterly.
A storm waits over the mountain.

❊   ❊   ❊

And no bird calls. Even the insects are long fled.
The air accepts the spirit of the scarecrow.
The only owl of the field is gone, or dead.
We would demand an explanation,
But what right do we have to one?
We are only the workers of the field,
Creatures of whatever substance these fields are made.
To know why the wheat will fall
Is to know why we have fallen."

"But should we accept this plight?"

"Can we know another?"

"We can build on what we know."

"All we know is
A storm waits over the mountain.
And no bird calls. Even the insects are long fled.
The air accepts the spirit of the scarecrow.
The only owl of the field is gone, or dead."

   Then the earthen figures crumbled,
And dust whirled across the land in a violent wind
   Under the fading illusion of the sky.

❋ ❋ ❋

IV

I think I can sometimes see
   The decay of a world
      within the world:

   Memories, a drifting loss,
   Sail the stream
   Like the last leaves of winter,
   Ice-embossed, in spring

   And they sail the stream
   Under a mist
   Like glistening steam

   And they sail the stream
   Into an ocean
   And the ocean is a star
   Like stars in a dream

   In the wide silver sanctuary of water
   The breaking waves part
      beneath the sleeping moon
   The mind
      from the fiery heart.

❋ ❋ ❋

A word is a world. In a world of words.
Understand that words offer nothing
But excuses for the seeds
Which have not been planted,
Or the ones which have fallen on stone.

Where am I in this wood of words
In my night?
The moon lingers bright.
Away.

Memory betrays
Bringing the apparition of a face into focus
When all you saw were blurred lips
        and a haze of eyes.

The betrayal?
    The golden branch lightening
        through dark depressing clouds.
    The glass-like dream of the key
        upon the table of an empty room.

Betrayal, the only hope?
    And the hope, too rare,
        like a certain kind of despair.
The lemon-breasted girl,

❋   ❋   ❋

The path winding through
Mist of dawn, thin vapors of dew,
And the ancient brick chimney
Are images that curl
Like snakes about my memory.

There, the oars of shipwrecked sailors
Bake in the sun-hot sand,
Splinters of wood that pierce
And will remain.
    And will remain
A darkness within me: who have patrolled the eyes
Of the nameless insane, hearing
The anguished whispers.

Where is there an end to the violent whirlpools
Of ocean fire, spewing only driftwood on the endless
Circuitous currents of the sea,
Amid the complacent faces of insinuating waves?
Only the driftwood, and the driftwood tangled in seaweed,
Ashes upon endless waters.

※　※　※

Ash of the sea,
    you drift to the shore
Where home is a defeat and a repeated prayer:
The broken oar
Bakes in the sun-hot sand.

V

Still is the child
Behind the glass
That questions me with a stare . . .

As when, at the end of a vacant afternoon,
The needle of the phonograph
Enters the vacant circle between two bands
And is received . . . I am stunned.
Silence, when music ends,
Is deeper than silence.

In paradisum . . .

The words proceed in the solemn cortege
Toward the silent shore
(Anchored ships, waiting in harbor)

Chaos is, at the perfect moment, drawn
Into the incorrigible heart of form.

✳ ✳ ✳

A restless purity in things revives the air
And prepares the day for its demise.

In the process of evening,
The sad quiet grayblue glow of a lingering day
Enters in sunwave processions
Through a bay window and an open door,
And on the mantle of the fireplace:
The antique sad sighs of a silent figure,
Arabesque of porcelain and gloom,
Dancing in glacial time,
Spinning a gray cocoon,
Out of the dying time,
And out of the dying room.

In the speculations of these idle hours,
Drawn out of day into figures of sleep,
There is the confusing fluency, yet instancy, of dream.
Pliant shapes slither on a faceless river.
But nothing is named. Nothing is known.

Home is a defeat and a repeated prayer.
Even in our arrival, as we return
We have not reached home. For home is
To wander.

❋　❋　❋

And that is what destroys us.
And that is what sustains us.

The oars of shipwrecked sailors
Bake in the sun-hot sand.

The decay of a world
                    within the world:
In the process of evening,
Anticipating the helpless delirium of age.

In the interpenetration of paradoxical visions,
The whole world becomes a graveyard where the tombs
And trees and flowers are made of mist
And refract the light of a sun
Just born, to give us infinite rainbows of that distant world
Which we sometimes hear beyond the despairing hymn
Of a violin, or which we feel
When the symphony and the air
Tremble together in the same clarity
And the hall itself seems suspended
In time or place from any mere position,
And the exit still hovering in music
Becomes a strange walk into a world we have forgotten
And are trying to remember.
                    Opinions overheard
In the numbed crowd reveal the failure

✳ ✳ ✳

Of the human instrument. The grating of the voices,
Of shoes on the dead concrete.

These splinters that pierce my heart.

On the dark lake, a hunter's light shines.
    Terror, *et terra gloria.*

I will go away, a child's rattle,
Shaken.

    Lux perpetua luceat eis.

Before I leave, I will turn back and stare
Into the glint of an infant eye, and see
The murmur of light from a withering star.

Epitaph

Epitaph

He made the book, and he died
As he had lived, forgetting,

He made the book as he defied
Those who said, *It's so unfitting*!

He made the book as he had made
Love to mad lovers (in the shade)

Until the last
Woman led him through his vanishing past.

He made everything to order
As he specified,

Except the soft evading grace
He found lasting in one face,

Making her love his staying world
Where he could sleep in kindness curled,

And all the world that he forgot
Returned—because it can not fade,

Returned transfigured out of fear and not
Forgotten like a book unmade.

DATE DUE